DISNEY
THE LITTLE MERMAID
ARIEL'S BEGINNING

Songs from the Heart

Adapted by Allison Lassieur

Cover illustrated by Elisa Marrucchi

Interior illustrated by Elizabeth Tate and the Disney Storybook Artists

A GOLDEN BOOK • NEW YORK

Copyright © 2008 Disney Enterprises, Inc. All rights reserved. Published in the United States by Golden Books, an imprint of Random House Children's Books, a division of Random House, Inc., 1745 Broadway, New York, NY 10019, and in Canada by Random House of Canada Limited, Toronto, in conjunction with Disney Enterprises, Inc. Golden Books, A Golden Book, and the G colophon are registered trademarks of Random House, Inc.

ISBN: 978-0-7364-2497-4

www.randomhouse.com/kids/disney

Printed in the United States of America

1 0 9 8 7 6 5 4 3 2

Under the sea lies a beautiful kingdom called Atlantica.

Young Princess Ariel loves King Triton very much.

Every night, Queen Athena sings a special song to Ariel
and her sisters.
Unscramble the letters to find out what kind
of song Queen Athena sings.

Y A L L L U B

_ _ _ _ _ _ _

King Triton gives the queen a beautiful music box.

Trace the lines to complete Queen Athena's special gift.

Ariel and her sisters love seeing their parents so happy.
Find the name of each princess in the puzzle below.
Look up, down, backward, forward, and diagonally.

A A N I T T A
R L L D A R T
I A D E L L A
S N I S I E U
T A N A R R Q
A N D R I N A

Arista • Alana • Ariel • Attina
Andrina • Adella • Aquata

ANSWER:

Look out—pirates!

The queen races to get her music box—
and swims straight into danger!

King Triton angrily bans all music from Atlantica!

Ten years later, Ariel wakes to the first sign of spring.

Marina Del Rey is the royal governess who takes care of the princesses. Benjamin is her kindhearted assistant.

"Uppy-uppy, my darlings!" says Marina.
Can you circle Marina's shadow?

A

B

C

D

Marina doesn't like taking care of the princesses.
"I hate this job!" she tells Benjamin.

Sebastian is King Triton's chief of staff.

How many sea horses can you count?

Every morning, the princesses take a walk with their father.
But Ariel wants to do something different.
"Not today!" replies King Triton.

Ariel tries to have fun while the princesses are
on their walk.

King Triton is very upset!

Triton punishes Ariel by making her scrape barnacles.
Can you count the barnacles?

Benjamin doesn't like feeding Marina's pets.

"Ooh, that Sebastian!" says Marina Del Rey.
She wants his job.
Connect the dots to find out whom Marina is complaining to.

Marina imagines herself as King Triton's new chief of staff.

As Ariel scrapes barnacles, she hears
something odd—music!

It's against the law to play music!
Palace guards catch the little fish.

"Hi, I'm Flounder," says the fish.
"I'm Ariel," says the Little Mermaid. They work together
to escape from the guards.

Ariel convinces Sebastian to let Flounder go.

Later, Triton comes to say good night.
Ariel is still upset about being punished.

Where is Flounder going?

Ariel follows Flounder to the secret door.
Can you help her choose the right path?

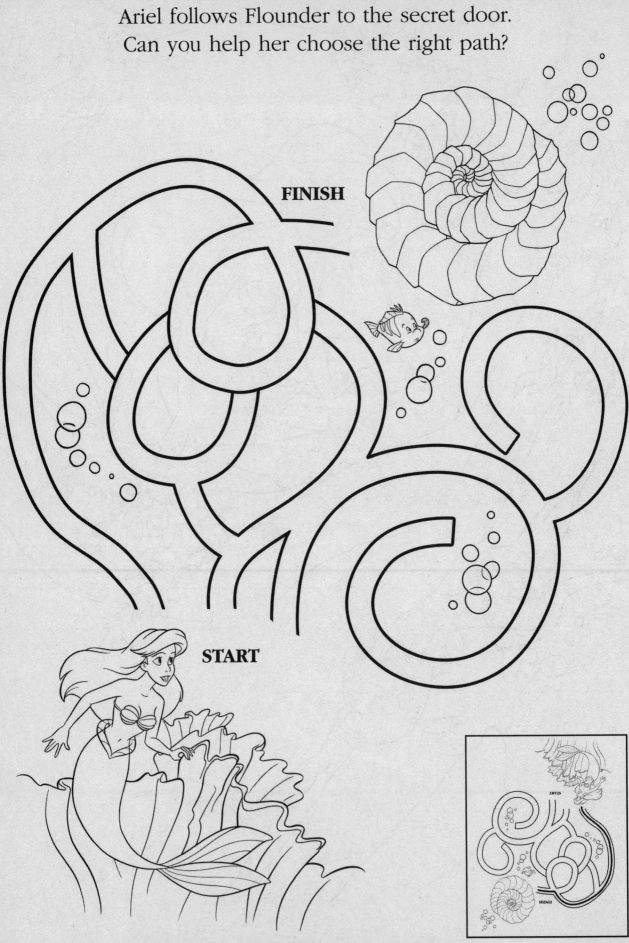

FINISH

START

Whoops!

Ariel is greeted by musical clams. She has entered a secret
nightclub called the Catfish Club!

Ariel is thrilled to find such a wonderful place.

The Catfish Club band is hopping tonight! Ink Spot
plays keyboards, Shelbow is on drums,
Cheeks plays the horn, and Ray-Ray plays the bass.

Look forward, backward, up, down, and diagonally to
find the names of all the band members
and their instruments.

```
R  C  C  A  E  H  T  W
A  V  H  O  N  O  R  O
Y  T  E  G  P  R  D  B
R  N  E  S  R  N  R  L
A  S  K  U  L  F  U  E
Y  N  S  S  A  B  M  H
I  K  O  P  S  B  S  S
K  E  Y  B  O  A  R  D
```

Ink Spot • Keyboard • Bass • Drums
Cheeks • Horn • Ray-Ray • Shelbow

ANSWER:

```
R  C  C  A  E  H  T  W
A  V  H  O  N  O  R  O
Y  T  E  G  P  R  D  B
R  N  E  S  R  N  R  L
A  S  K  U  L  F  U  E
Y  N  S  S  A  B  M  H
I  K  O  P  S  B  S  S
K  E  Y  B  O  A  R  D
```

The Catfish Club's star performer is not happy to see Ariel!
Connect the dots to see who is the club's star.

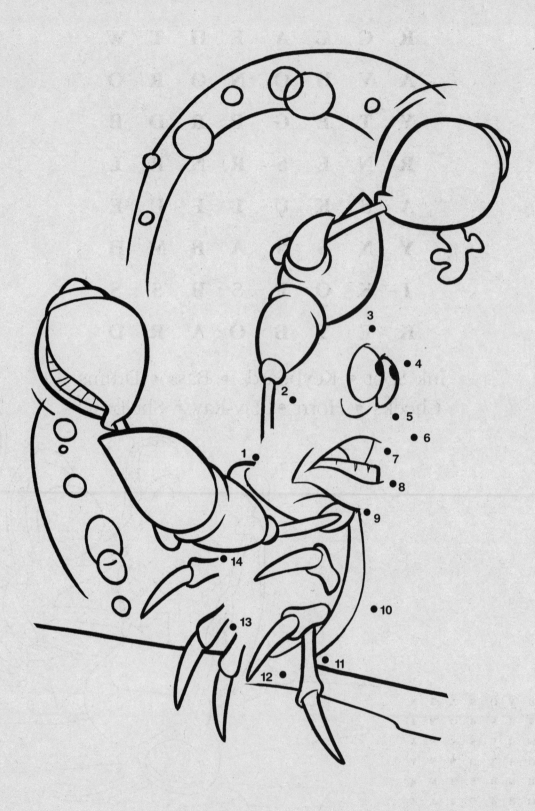

"Wait! I won't tell!" calls Ariel. But everyone swims away.

For the first time in ten years, Ariel sings her
mother's lullaby. It makes her feel better.

Everyone in the Catfish Club comes back.
They love Ariel's singing!

Ariel takes the musician's oath—to always help her
fellow music lovers!

What does Triton order Sebastian to do?
Finish the phrase by filling in the vowel A, E, I, O, or U.

W __ T C H __ R __ __ L

ANSWER: Watch Ariel.

Ariel's sisters want to go to the Catfish Club, too!

The next night, all the princesses have a great time
at the Catfish Club!

All the princesses' beds are empty.
Where is everyone?

Marina sees Sebastian and the princesses making music at the club. Which band member is helping Arista play the horn? Trace the lines to find out.

Marina tells King Triton about the Catfish Club.

"This is how you watch over my daughter?"
Triton asks Sebastian.

"Lock them all away!" orders the king.
Triton makes Marina his new chief of staff.

King Triton destroys the Catfish Club!
Circle the words that describe how he is feeling.

mad   calm   happy   angry   glad

upset   quiet   furious

ANSWER: King Triton is feeling mad, angry, upset, and furious.

"I will not have music in my kingdom!"
King Triton shouts.

"I may not remember much about my mother, but I know she wouldn't have wanted this!" Ariel says.

Marina is very happy. Soon she'll have all the power
she has ever wanted!

The music Ariel loved is gone. The blossom is the only
beautiful thing in her world now.
How many blossoms are in the picture?

Triton misses Athena.
Help him find his way through the garden to
the statue of the royal couple.

FINISH

START

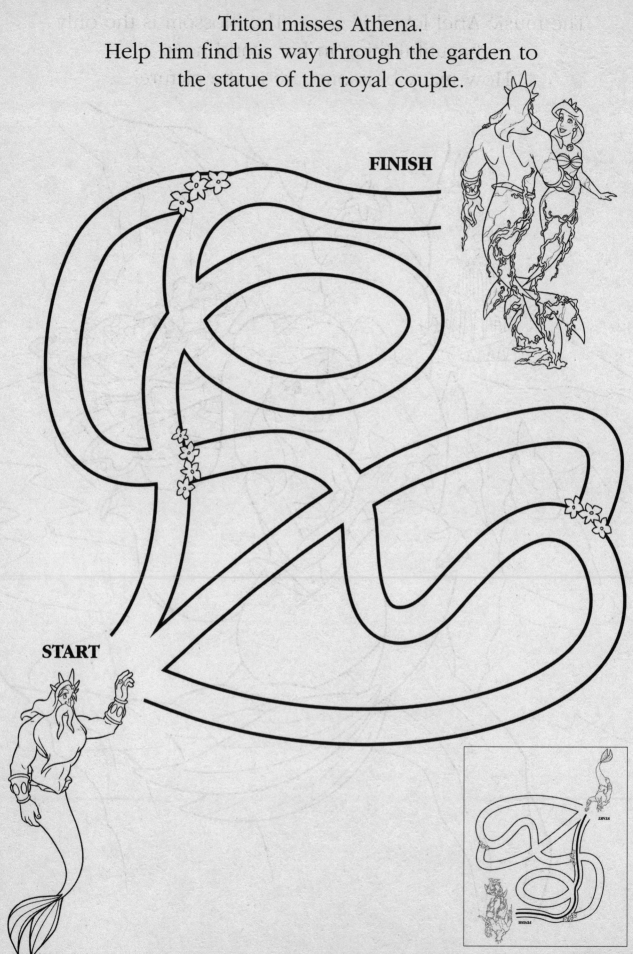

Ariel decides to run away.

The band is in the dungeon.

"Come on," Ariel says. "Let's go!"

"Without music, Atlantica just isn't home," Ariel says.

Away from Atlantica, the band lets loose!

Benjamin makes a discovery.

King Triton wonders if he was too hard on Sebastian
and the girls.

"Ariel is missing!" cries Attina. "We've looked everywhere!"

Triton is very worried.
Unscramble the letters to read his command.

I D N F   L E I A R

_ _ _ _   _ _ _ _ _ !

Sebastian leads the band to a strange place
they have never seen.

"There's more to this place than meets the eye,"
Sebastian says.

Marina doesn't want to lose her new job!
She has a plan but needs Benjamin's key.

"Who wants crab cakes?" asks Marina.
Connect the dots to find out whom Marina orders
to get rid of Sebastian.

As Ariel wakes up, she hears something. . . .

Where is the music coming from?
Help Ariel find the right path to the music.

FINISH

START

ANSWER:

Ariel recognizes the music box.

It's the music box that Triton gave to Athena!

"When your mother died, the whole kingdom was heartbroken," says Sebastian. Ariel realizes that her father has forgotten how to be happy.

Ariel wants to take something back to her father in Atlantica. To find out what it is, cross out every L and T. Then write the letters that are left in order on the lines below.

LTMLUTSTLICT

LBLOLTXL

_ _ _ _ _ _   _ _ _

The band doesn't want to go back to Atlantica.
The musicians don't want to be arrested again.

Ariel and Sebastian head back to Atlantica.

"Hey, Ariel, wait up!" calls Flounder.

Eels are hiding in the kelp forest!
How many eels can you count?

ANSWER: 4.

"Surprise!" cackles Marina Del Rey. She doesn't want Ariel
and her friends to return home.

Ariel, Sebastian, and Flounder escape the eels.

It's an undersea showdown! Sebastian wins this round.

Marina fights back!

Ariel and Flounder are trapped!

The band comes to the rescue!
Musicians help other musicians.

Marina can't wait to get her hands on Sebastian!

"I win!" cries Sebastian.

Flounder tries a tricky move with the eels.

Flounder's plan works.
How many eels are twisted together?

ANSWER: 3.

But Marina won't give up. Ariel rushes to help Sebastian.

King Triton arrives just in time to see Ariel in danger.

"What have I done?" Triton asks sadly. He begins to sing softly along with the music box, trying to comfort Ariel.

"Daddy, let's go home," Ariel says.

After they return home, Sebastian is named court composer—
and King Triton takes the musician's oath!

Once again, Atlantica is filled with laughter, love, and music . . .

. . . even in the dungeon!